For Gabriella, Duncan, and Ana and all the cool trips ahead.
Special thanks to Maria.

Splat and the Cool School Trip
Copyright © 2013 by Rob Scotton
All rights reserved. Printed in the United States of America.
No part of this book may be used or reproduced in any manner whatsoever without
written permission except in the case of brief quotations embodied in critical articles
and reviews. For information address HarperCollins Children's Books, a division of
HarperCollins Publishers, 10 East 53rd Street, New York, NY 10022.
www.harpercollinschildrens.com
Library of Congress Cataloging-in-Publication Data is available.
ISBN 978-0-06-213386-1
Typography by Jeanne L. Hogle
13 14 15 16 17 LP 10 9 8 7 6 5 4 3 2 1
❖
First Edition

Splat and the Cool School Trip

Rob Scotton

HARPER
An Imprint of HarperCollinsPublishers

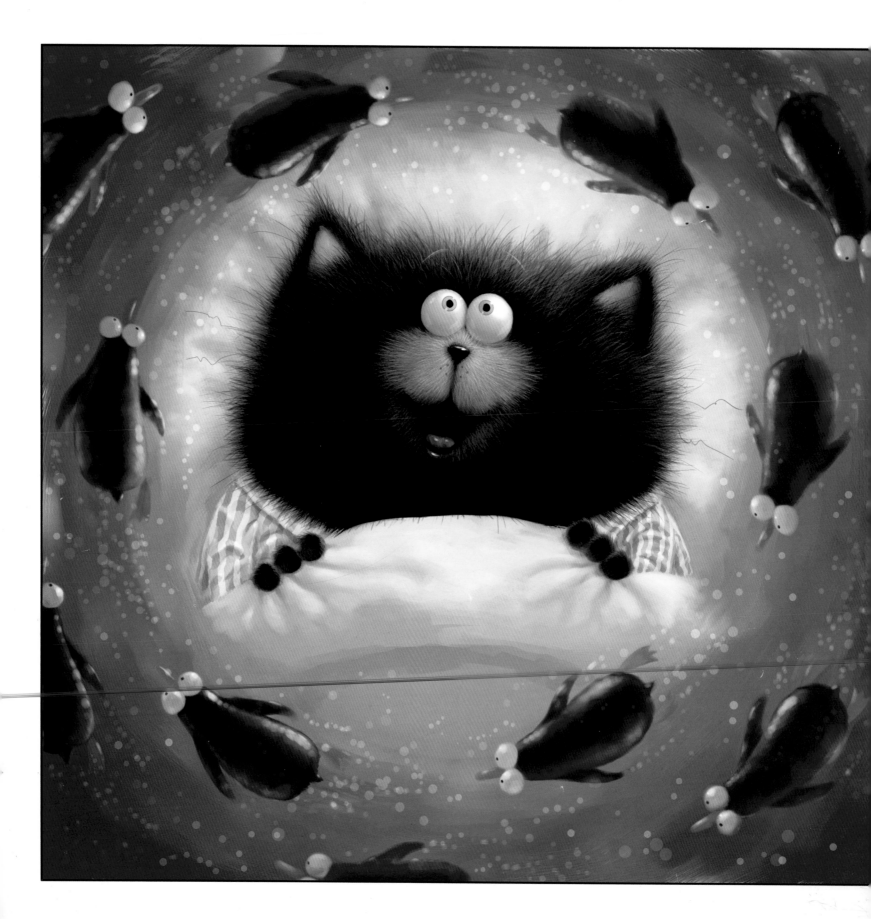

"It's Penguin Day!"

cried Splat

as he woke from his favorite dream.

Splat's class was going to the zoo.

And Splat was too excited to sleep.

"I can't wait to see the penguins," said Splat.

"They have big round eyes and walk with a waddle.
They're the best!" he added.
Seymour nodded.

Splat got ready for school.

"Did you know penguins love to swim?" asked Splat.
Seymour nodded.

Then Splat remembered
something Mrs. Wimpydimple said.

"You can't come because mice scare
the elephants," said Splat.

"I'm sorry, Seymour."

So Splat went to school, leaving a disappointed Seymour behind.

But Seymour wanted to go to the zoo.
And he had a plan.

hehehe

Flying for Dummies

Flying for Dummies

MAKING STUFF FROM PAPER

Flying
for
Dummies

At Cat School, after Splat and his class boarded the bus, Mrs. Wimpydimple asked a question.

"Which animal is your favorite?"

"The giraffe," said Plank. "He's really tall."

"The monkey," said Kitten. "She's so cute."

"The elephant," said Spike. "He's so strong."

"Penguins!" cried Splat.
"I can't wait to see the penguins."

The bus rattled along the road . . .

. . . and soon arrived at the zoo.
"Let's go and *see* the penguins first!" cried Splat.
"Later, Splat!" Mrs. Wimpydimple sighed.

OTHER ANIMALS

TO THE PENGUINS

"I can't wait!" said Splat.

"Look, a giraffe," said Plank.
"He can reach the high branches."

"Look, a monkey," cried Kitten.
"She's so furry."

"Look, an elephant," said Spike.
"He's so strong."
"They're cool," sighed Splat.
"But they're not penguins."

Splat looked up and pointed at something in the sky.
"Is it a bird?" he asked. "No!" cried the cats.

"Is it a plane?" he asked. "Well, sort of!" cried the cats.

"It's Seymour!"

Seymour waved but then lost his balance . . .
and crashed into the elephant.

"Uh-oh!" said Splat.

Seymour stared at the elephant.
The elephant stared at Seymour.

And then . . . "MOUSE!" cried the elephant.

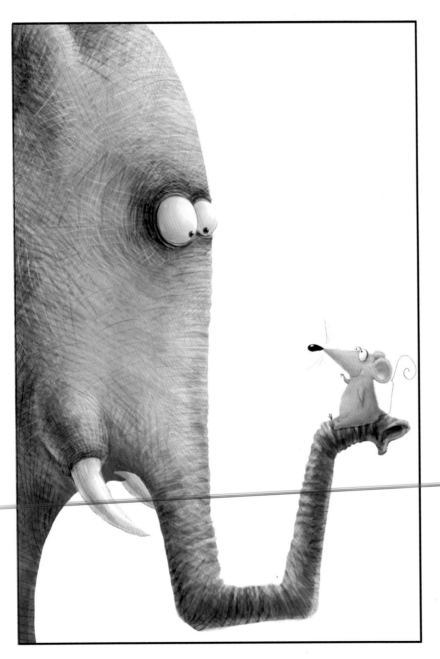

"Uh-oh!" said Splat.

The elephant was so frightened he trumpeted,
ran away, and jumped over a wall.

"I guess Mrs. Wimpydimple was right," said Splat.
"Elephants are afraid of mice."

The class continued around the zoo until they finally arrived at the . . .

Penguin Pool

"Hurrah!" cheered Splat.

But Splat's hurrah didn't last long.
A sign on the wall read:

Due to an elephant
breaking the pool
the Penguins cannot
come out today.
Sorry!

CAT SCHOOL

"What! No penguins?" said Splat.

"No penguins!" said Mrs. Wimpydimple.
"Everybody back to the bus."

Splat was so disappointed.

Seymour was dismayed.
It was his fault that Splat couldn't *see* the penguins.

So he thought about how he could make things right.

He peeked into the penguin house. Without any water
to swim in, all the penguins were huddled inside.

Seymour had an idea.
"Hmm," he said. "Follow me."

And they did. . . .

The bus rattled back to Cat School.

Splat wandered home.

ssshhh...

Played with his dinner.

Stared at the TV.

And then went to bed.

But Splat couldn't sleep.

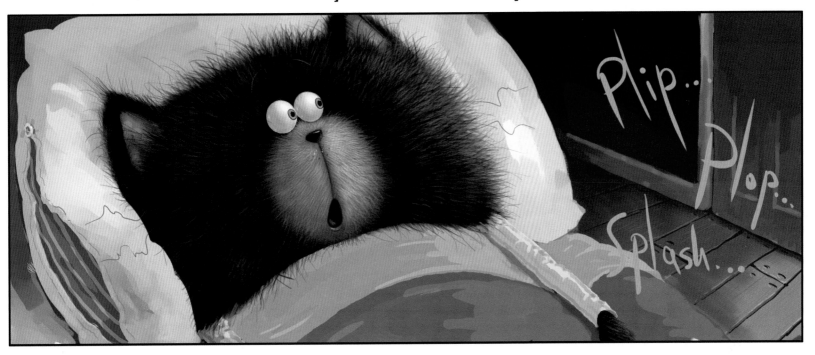

He heard a splashing noise coming from the bathroom.
It got louder.

He decided to investigate.

Something was moving behind the shower curtain.
He gulped.

Splat pulled the shower curtain open.

And to his amazement . . .

"Penguins!" he cried.

"It's Penguin Day after all."